I'm a Weaned Kid Now!

by Kristi Patrice Carter, J.D.

Illustrated by Avoltha

ISBN-13: 978-1517793708
ISBN-10: 151779370X

This is a work of fiction. Names, characters, places, and incidents either are the product of the author's imagination or are used fictitiously. Any resemblance to actual persons, living or dead, events, or locales is entirely coincidental. Readers are reminded to use their own good judgment before applying any ideas presented in this fiction book.

Thang Publishing Company
332 South Michigan Avenue
Suite 1032-T610
Chicago, Illinois 60604-4434
800-441-9026

For additional assistance with the weaning process, please visit http://www.weaningthang.com or purchase **Wean that Kid: Your Comprehensive Guide to Understanding and Mastering the Weaning Process**, now available at http://www.amazon.com.

Acknowledgements

I'd like to give a special thanks to:

My loving husband Delanza Shun-tay Carter, for encouraging me to write this book, for being supportive about nursing our three children and patient throughout the weaning process, and for unwaveringly and lovingly playing with the kids so that I could complete this book.

My daughter Kristin Carter and my sons Shaun Carter and Daniel Carter, for teaching me the wonders of motherhood, allowing me to share the joys of nursing, and helping me to overcome the challenges of weaning.

My mom Christina Tarr, who supported my nursing decision, assisted with the weaning process, and unselfishly came over as needed to watch the kids so that I could write this guide.

My father Lavon Tarr, for loving me and not complaining when Mom came over.

My aunt Mary Turner and cousin Alison Turner-Graham (who is like a sister) for their support during the weaning process.

I would like to thank Avoltha for her beautiful illustrations; Alex, my graphic designer who designed my dynamic e-book cover; and Amy Shelby, for her proofreading assistance.

I would also like to give my heartfelt thanks to all the mothers and children who are breastfeeding, considering weaning or going through the weaning process. I understand your weaning challenges and share in your weaning triumphs. Hopefully, Chloe's mother-led weaning experience will assist with this transitional phase.

This book is dedicated to Kristin, Shaun, and Daniel Carter, and Austin Graham.

Hello, Friends! My name is Chloe and I'm a weaned kid! Weaning is not so bad, and guess what? You can be a weaned kid too!

I sat in Mommy's lap and tried to nurse.

Mommy said, "Chloe, I love you very much. But you are getting older. It is time for you to be weaned."

I didn't know what 'weaned' meant, but it sounded scary.

Mommy told me that when you are a baby, your body can't handle foods like bread, fruits, vegetables, and meat. So, you either drink milk from Mommy's milkies or baby formula. She also told me that when you get older, your body can handle big kid foods and you don't need your Mommy's milkies anymore.

Mommy said that being weaned means that you drink your milk from a cup instead of Mommy's milkies. That made me very sad.

I like to drink my juice from my cup, but Mommy doesn't hold me and cuddle me and tell me she loves me when I drink my juice. Milk from Mommy's milkies is warm and yummy! Milk in a cup is cold and yucky.

When Mommy told me it was time to start weaning, I was both mad and sad. I didn't want to start weaning that day. Mommy told me that it would be fine and that I'd be a weaned kid soon.

When Mommy gave me my milk in a cup, I threw it down and made a big mess. I didn't want to be mean but I didn't want to drink milk in a cup. I wanted to drink milk from Mommy's yummy milkies.

I started to cry and couldn't stop. Mommy looked very sad but she told me that I shouldn't have thrown my cup of milk on the floor. She told me to go to my room for a while and think about how I could have acted nicer.

I didn't want Mommy to be sad or mad at me, but I just wasn't happy. I didn't feel like being nice. I wanted Mommy's milkies.

I went to my room, hugged my blankie, and cried and cried. But even that didn't make me feel better.

Soon, my daddy came into my room. "What's wrong, Princess Chloe? Why did you throw your milk on the floor?" My daddy always calls me his princess. That usually makes me smile but it didn't that day. I couldn't stop crying so he sat on my bed and hugged me really tight.

After a little while, I felt better. I told Daddy I was sad because I didn't want to stop drinking milk from Mommy's yummy milkies. I wanted to be close to Mommy. I love her so much. And I love her milk.

Daddy told me not to worry. He said, "Mommy and I love you very much, Princess Chloe. You can always be close to Mommy and snuggle with her, even if you are a weaned kid. But you can't throw things like your milk, Princess Chloe. It's not nice at all. "

Then Mommy came to my room. I told her I was very sorry for throwing my cup of milk on the floor. She picked me up and hugged me. She told me she understood how I felt and that getting weaned would take time. She told me that I could do it. She told me that I could do anything if I put my mind to it. I felt much better then.

Mommy held me close and reminded me that I don't have to nurse to be close to her. She said, "I will hold you anytime you need to be close to me, Chloe. I will rock you. I will sing to you. I will talk to you. I will always love you."

Daddy brought us both a cup of milk. At first, the milk in the cup was kind of cold. I didn't like that so Daddy warmed it for me. It tasted really good then.

After Mommy and I finished our milk, Daddy told me, "Princess Chloe, when you don't have to nurse as much, we can go to really neat places a lot more often. You can do big girl things like fishing, skating, and riding a bike."

I love to ride in Daddy's big truck. I love to go fishing and swimming with him. I've always wanted to ride a big girl bike like my cousin Alison. She is 4 and has a really cool two-wheel bike with training wheels.

After snack time, Daddy and I went to the playground to have fun together. He pushed me on the swing really high and he caught me at the end of the big slide that all the big kids play on. I love Daddy so much.

Mommy used to nurse me in the morning. She nursed me at snack time. She nursed me at naptime. She nursed me at bedtime. She nursed me when I was sad or thirsty. She nursed me when I needed to be close to her. Mommy told me we would stop nursing a little at a time so it would not be so hard for me to be weaned.

First, we stopped nursing in the morning.

That wasn't so hard because mornings were usually very busy for us anyway. In the morning, Mommy made me breakfast. We had pancakes and I had milk in a box with a straw (she called the box a "carton"). It was pretty neat.

On special days, Mommy made me chocolate or strawberry milk. I can't have too much of that because it is really sweet, but it is really yummy. Mommy told me her milk doesn't have flavors in it.

When we finished eating, Mommy sat with me. She cuddled me and tickled me while we watched cartoons. She told me she loved me. She told me she was proud of me. That was so much fun.

I used to nurse before lunch but now Mommy gives me a big hug and kiss instead. Sometimes I have fruit or veggies (I love carrots and celery) for a yummy snack.

I soon got used to not nursing in the morning and before lunch. It was not so bad. Then, a few weeks later, Mommy told me we were going to cut out nursing at NAPTIME! I didn't like that idea at all. I thought about crying and stomping my feet. But I didn't. I told Mommy how I felt. I used my big girl words.

Mommy held me close but didn't nurse me.

Mommy told me that she loves me.

Mommy read me a story about growing up.

Mommy rocked me to sleep.

Soon, I didn't miss nursing after lunch.

But it was really hard when we quit nursing at night. Mommy used to nurse me to sleep. Then, Daddy started to rock me to sleep. It was nice to be close to Daddy, but I missed Mommy's yummy milkies. I missed Mommy but I enjoyed time with Daddy.

When I couldn't fall asleep and I cried for Mommy, she came to my room. She didn't nurse me though. But she gave me a big hug and lots of kisses.

She told me she loved me.

She told me a story about a big girl named Chloe and all the great things she would do when she was a weaned kid.

She kissed me and sang me a song.

She hugged me.

She rubbed my back until I fell asleep.

It didn't take long until I learned to fall asleep that way.

Then, something really cool happened. One bright morning Mommy told me, "Chloe, I have great news for you. You are finally weaned. You haven't nursed for over two weeks. We're going to have a big girl birthday and weaning party for you because we're so proud of you!"

We had a big party at my house. All of my friends and family came to tell me that they were proud of me being a big kid. We had cupcakes, cake, and milk in cartons with colored straws. As a special surprise, I got a two-wheel bike like Alison's. It was pink and green and had streamers on the handlebars. It also had cool training wheels.

Being a weaned kid is so much fun!

Now I really like being a weaned kid. Mommy and Daddy are so proud of me, and I'm proud too!

Now that I'm weaned, Mommy still cuddles me a lot, reads to me, and sings to me. Daddy takes me to lots of new places and plays with me a lot too. I've even learned to ride my new bike.

However, no matter how big I get, I will always love Mommy and Daddy and I know they will love me too.

Sometimes I still miss Mommy's milkies, but when I start to feel that way, I go to Mommy and she gives me a big hug and lots of kisses and makes me feel so much better. I tell Daddy how I feel and he hugs me too.

I love being a weaned kid now!

You can be a weaned kid too!

Bonus Section for Parents

Weaning Affirmations

and

50 Activities You Can Do With Your Child During the Weaning Process

(Excerpted from Wean that Kid by Kristi Patrice Carter, J.D. –
now available on Amazon.com)

Weaning Affirmations for Moms

My baby knows that I love her and she will get all of the nourishment she needs from her food.

The bond that I have developed with my baby will not go away; it will change and grow into a beautiful new bond, like a butterfly coming out of a cocoon.

My body is open to this next stage of my child's development and I am ready for this process.

My partner is ready to be more actively involved in the nourishment of our child. This is my gift to both of them.

Weaning is a natural part of my child's growth and development. We are both ready for this next step.

Gradually weaning my baby is what's best for both of us. We can ease into this in a natural rhythm.

My child is ready for this. This transition will be a positive, beautiful transition.

I have a newfound sense of freedom in this next stage of our life. I will embrace all of the opportunities for love and laughter that are placed before me.

Roller coasters of emotion are a natural part of this process. I will move through them gracefully and know that laughing and exercising are natural remedies to help me find an emotional balance.

I will give myself extra love and care during this time of changes in my life.

50 Fun Activities to Do With Your Child During the Weaning Process (Excerpt from Wean that Kid)

1. Make a big, soft, safe pile of cushions, pillows, comforters, and other soft bedding. Let your child roll around and jump in the pile.

2. Make finger puppets by cutting off the fingers of old pairs of gloves. Draw funny faces on them and put on a show for your child.

3. Make a sock puppet out of an old sock and put it on your child's hand so he or she can make it move.

4. Drape a sheet over a table or the backs of two chairs and make a tent. Camp out under the tent with your child.

5. Give your child a clean rag or dish towel and allow him or her to "clean" the floor.

6. Play peek-a-boo.

7. Read aloud, using big books with large pictures. It's never too early to start reading to and with your child!

8. Visit the grocery store together. Put your child in the shopping cart's child seat and let him or her feel, see, and smell the different items you are buying.

9. Have fun walking around backwards and sideways.

10. In the autumn, go outside and try to catch falling leaves.

11. In the winter, try to catch falling snowflakes.

12. In the spring or summer, blow bubbles with a bubble-wand and let your child try to catch them.

13. Play with building blocks.

14. See how high you can build a structure before it tumbles down.

15. Take turns making funny noises.

16. Give your child a beach ball and sit opposite him or her on the floor. Hold out a large basket, such as a laundry basket or clean garbage can, and let your child try to throw the ball into the basket.

17. Shake a big sheet over your head like a parachute and let it fall on top of you both.

18. In the bathtub, give your child an empty can or bucket. Let him or her fill up the container and pour it out.

19. Take a nap with your child, or simply enjoy some quiet time in bed.

20. Sing a song to your young one.

21. Give your child a stuffed animal and ask him or her to "tuck it into bed."

22. Turn on the radio and move around to the music.

23. Visit the children's section of your local library for story time.

24. Play dress-up.

25. Put out paper and large crayons and have fun scribbling away!

26. Do large cardboard puzzles.

27. String large beads on thread or cord (supervise children carefully to make sure they don't swallow the beads!).

28. Play shadow puppets with a flashlight on a wall.

29. Go to the zoo.

30. When you get home from the zoo, make up a story with your child about one of the animals you saw.

31. Take a walk. On the way, point out interesting sights, animals, houses, clouds, or plants.

32. Go to the park and play on the swing set.

33. Go to a local art museum or gallery and have your child point out his or her favorite paintings or sculptures.

34. If you live near the seashore, pack a picnic lunch and eat it on the beach.

35. Give your child a piggyback ride.

36. Read a book together.

37. Make funny faces in a mirror. Get out a camera and take turns snapping pictures of each other.

38. Watch an educational program, such as *Sesame Street*, together.

39. Have a casual meal at a family restaurant.

40. Make musical instruments out of pots, pans, and spoons.

41. Buy or make some play dough (you can find lots of easy recipes on the web!) and let your child make shapes and then mush them up.

42. Ask your child to help you make breakfast. Make smiley-face pancakes by decorating them with chocolate chips or blueberries.

43. Skip down the hall or in the backyard.

44. Get out paper and crayons and draw portraits of each other and objects around the house.

45. Make up and sing silly songs together.

46. Have your child help you with tasks around the house. For example, have him or her help you pick up toys and throw trash in the wastebasket.

47. Turn on the radio and have a dance contest.

48. Play make-believe. Pretend that you are at the beach or in a strange new forest.

49. Make a special trip to the library to get your child his or her library card.

50. Splash through puddles and mud together after a big rainstorm. Make a big mess of yourselves, and then come indoors, clean up, and sip hot cocoa or chocolate milk.

Need more assistance with the weaning process? Please purchase **Wean that Kid: Your Comprehensive Guide to Understanding and Mastering the Weaning Process**, now available at http://www.http://amzn.to/1NvHk3o. Or, you can visit http://www.weaningthang.com, a comprehensive site that provides breastfeeding and weaning support, articles, reviews, videos, and tools to make the breastfeeding and weaning process easier.

Made in United States
Troutdale, OR
03/27/2024

18773806R00019